Rush

Of

Many

Waters

Also by Pauly Hart

Rush of Many Waters:
Volume Twenty
By Pauly Hart

Contents

Shorts

Wall Man

Roy -

The diner was shut down, but Roy thought he heard it again. A dull clink and a thud. Was that Ice maker messing up again? Dammit! He pulled up his pants and shut the laptop. Red Tube would have to wait. No sense scaring Consuelo or Raoul while they were cleaning. He left the office, turned right and pushed the service door to the kitchen open with a bang. Both cleaners jumped and Consuelo dropped the mop.

"Did you guys mess with the ice maker?" he asked, a little hotly.

"Eh. No senor, we don't clean this." Raoul pointed to the icemaker. It was in the back corner, next to the salad prep area, by the expo table.

"Dammit," Roy thought. The ice machine was a piece of junk and it was always acting up. Just then, as if on cue, a load fell out and splashed to the bottom. It sat and slowly became part of the semi-frozen slush at the bottom. It would take all night to fill up, and that's all they really needed at this point. With the seven booths and six bar stations, they would be able to get through yet another day.

Money. It was always about money.

"Alright." He waived his hands absently at the two workers, cleaning the kitchen at their own slow pace. It's good that he had contracted these two out, and they weren't on the clock. They were slow as molasses.

Hmmm, speaking of molasses... Roy went back to the office to check his latest truck order, wondering if he had messed it up again.

"Hey did you guys do the restrooms already?" he called, as he walked out.

"Si!" they both said at once.

"Alright fine. I'll be in the office." he said, and walked out the right hand door, then left to the office, where he shut the door and locked it behind him.

Consuelo -

She didn't like Mister Roy. She knew that he looked at the naughty websites in the office when they cleaned. She knew there wasn't that much to do in there. And she had seen the way that he had looked at her. Pervertido. Mother Mary help us. Raoul pretended that it didn't matter. But he was a cholo, a banger. What did he know about the suffering of the Meztizos in Oklahoma? Whatever. She cleaned every day and it was a good job. And Roy didn't try to touch her. She would work hard and maybe they would give her more money. That was the way.

Raoul -

"Clean the stove. Clean the floors. Another dollar, another chore."

Funny. He should remember to add that in to a rap. He was getting pretty good at it in English. He still liked rapping in his native Espanol but sometimes the rhyme schemes were better in Gringo.

"Hey I got ta take out the trash... And it ain't cash..."

Naw homie.

He would get better. Then he could make a couple more tracks and put an album together. Then maybe he could get on a label, make that green, and all the ladies would be after him.

Not Consuelo though. She was his cousin's friend. She had a nice badonkadonk, but she was too old fashioned. No way Jose'. I ain't marrying un mamacita.

"She ain't my cuz, it's what it was..."

Restaurant -

"Alright you guys, have a good night!" Roy said as he walked the two workers out through the front door. It was a little cold outside and the wind whistled through into the main entryway, between booths two and three. Roy locked the door behind them and went back to the office. If you stood outside, and a little to the left of the front doors, you could see inside the office. Roy always shut the door. He would finish off his tantric episode with a moan of disgust and waddle to the restroom to clean up. Sometimes he cleaned up in the kitchen, in the summer, where it was sometimes still light outside. This was especially dreadful, because that's where the food was kept.

When Roy exited the restroom, he went to the thermostat and turned it down to 55 Fahrenheit. He thought he saved money like this, but all he really did was make the furnace work all the harder when they opened up the next morning. Roy was a fool and Restaurant knew it. The Thermostat was directly by the walk-in fridge, which was directly behind the bar, in the middle of the floorplan. It had been placed there for convenience so that the hood vent could be on an outside wall, but it never helped keep the heat.

When the clock struck two in the morning, the grate moved, and the prep table moved away from the wall. The shadow went to the kitchen door and peeked out. No one was in the parking lot in front, and there were no lights on the road. But precaution is always in his blood. He didn't take chances. He slid along the floor behind the bar and went to the restroom for his nightly shower and defecation. When that was finished around 2:08 AM (he scrubbed behind his ears today) he cleaned up and went to the kitchen. No booze today. He only did that on new bottles and the bar had been slow this last week.

Entering the kitchen, he went to the salad station and got some cucumbers, then to the walk-in, with a plate, and got some tuna. Snagging a bottle of water, he was back behind the prep table by 2:15. A slight shudder went through the room as he slid the table back into place.

Mandie -

The phone rang as she was turning on the computer.

Judge Thompson was on the... No, wait, his wife was... Wait. What?

"Alright, thank you Ruby, I'll make sure and let him know. No. No, I don't think it was anything here. No. Alri- Alright. Yes. Yes, you too. Bye now."

Weird. She turned on the monitor and opened up the clock-in program.

"Four years today." she thought, looking at the computer screen. Roy had left his laptop here again, and she had moved it to the side. She didn't want to know what was on the screen... A little afraid to look. Maybe furry porn this time. Gross. Everything that dude did was gross. At least he didn't hit on her anymore. That was a relief. He had a way with strangers that always came off as professional. But you had better stay a stranger. The more you got to know him, the grosser he became.

"I wish this place had benefits." she said out loud. It was a breath to the air, a plea to the unknown, she knew it. She lived off of tips and did pretty well. Her regulars loved the way that she made them feel, and they showed it in green. "Almost stripper money." She laughed. She had made bank when she worked at "Pleasers" down on Lewis Avenue, but that was so, so degrading. She liked her life better now that she was the head server here.

Roy called her "The Show." Not a bad name. It was better than "Candy" when she used to take her clothes off. Yesterday at lunch she made $142 in cash and $70 on Credit in tips. She always reported low, so that she could still get WIC for her two little girls.

They were her life, and she'd do anything for them.

Jeff -

"Mandie was already here. Good. Hopefully she turned up the heat already," he thought. He banged on the door and she saw him and came to the door.

"Hey there!" she said and opened the door.

"Roy wants tuna on the special today, but I don't know if we have enough." she started.

"Woah there. I haven't even had my coffee." he replied. He hated chipper people. It was only nine in the morning and they didn't open up until eleven thirty. Plenty of time to "rise and shine" as morning people liked to say. He could rise alright, but it took a while to shine.

Linda -

She put the bus tub full of tuna one shelf up, so she could better see them. Did they look a little green? Nah. It was just the light in here. Twelve.

"Hey Jeff! It says we should have fifteen tuna but we only have twelve!" she shouted from the Walk-in.

"Check again" he yelled back. She knew that he knew that she could hear him, but she just wanted to be annoying. He was such a grumpy-pants.

"WHAT?" she yelled, opening the door.

He rolled his eyes and threw his head back and said loudly "I said check again!"

She laughed and went back in, letting the door shut behind her. There it was, the order count from last night, says they should have fifteen. But (counting again), yup, there were only twelve in the bus tub.

She walked out with the tub and whacked it down on the expo table, with more force than she needed, to prove a point.

"Well do YOU want to count them?" she asked. "See?" Holding up three in each hand and slamming them on the counter. "Six plus six is NOT fifteen poop-head."

Jeff laughed at her and told her to tell Mandie, which she did.

Kevin -

Just setting up the bar, don't look over at her. Don't look... Shit. I looked. There was Linda, looking hotter than hell in all black. Man he needed some of that. He was almost done setting up the bar, cleaning the sink out, pouring chemicals out, cleaning out fruit flies from the Blue Curacao, and now it was ice time. He grabbed a bus tub from under the bar. His station could fit around two bus tubs full of ice, but he usually only did the shift with one. Today was Friday. He figured he would need two.

Abdul -

"Eh, Jeff! Something es wrong with thee Ice maker!" He was staring into it, as Kevin brought out the slush that was at the bottom.

"I tinka we need a new wonn man." Abdul said.

"Yeah man, this stinks too!" Kevin added.

Jeff walked over and cursed. He handed Abdul twenty and asked him to go to the gas station and bring back five big bags.

Abdul did as he was told. The gas station was only two buildings down, so he could make two trips to get it. Not a problem. He was a good worker. Everyone knew it. He always showed up early and worked some before he clocked in. Mister Roy yelled at him some, but he would know that Abdul was no slouch. Is that the word? Slouch? He would remember to ask Mandie if it was the right word. Mandie liked him. He was a hard worker.

After the second trip, and dumping them in, he handed Jeff the receipt, because Jeff always liked receipts. He always gave them to Mister Roy. He had seen it. He supposed that Jeff wanted to be paid back maybe. Abdul would have paid for it. Abdul was a good and honest worker. Not like

Jeff. Jeff might have the run of the kitchen, but Abdul would out-work him and take over his job. To have job security like this was a good thing. It was his dream to run his own kitchen.

Abdul noticed that Kevin had been right. The ice machine really did smell. He would tell Jeff.

Roy -

Roy wandered in at 11:15, in time for the last minute hustle and bustle of the setup. He had to use his key because everyone was in the kitchen, he guessed. He yelled his normal yell to get someone's attention.

"Yo!" he called. No one came.

Mandie popped out of the kitchen and waved frantically. "Roy! You gotta see this!" she said, and went back in.

"Dammit, what now?" he wondered. Opening the kitchen door, he saw everyone crowded around the ice machine. They had moved it away from the wall and put it against the expo table, the prep table was over by the hand washing station, and there was garbage all over the floor.

"What the hell guys!? We open in fifteen minutes!" he screamed. He could not believe this.

"What is all that stuff?" he demanded.

Just then, Linda turned away sharply and threw up in the handwashing station.

"Oh Gawd." she said.

All over the floor was moldy trash. A blanket, some clothes, gray and wrinkled, and a green pillow that looked like it at one time had been white.

Mandie grabbed Roy's arm and opened her mouth to speak but Jeff was quicker.

"There's a fucking hole in the wall Roy! A fucking hole!" He waived his hands.

"WHAT?" Roy shouted.

Just then, Kevin said: "Holy Shit! There's a guy in here!"

Restaurant -

I opened seven years ago. Wall man has been here ever since.

The last day of the installation, he had been working fitting the ice machine into the floor drain and they had locked him inside the room. He panicked, and no one remembered that he was there, as no one really liked him. So he stayed. He stole things here and there, a small pillow someone had left for their hemorrhoids, a coat, some clothes, and every day, some food. Never the same thing twice, so no one could become suspicious of anything, because he ate a very varied diet... As much as this tiny restaurant could afford to give him.

One of the finishing crew that installed the plumbing, he had been one of the last people to work on the rough-out on the renovation. The space originally had been for a small drain, but they weren't going to use that space, so they just boxed it in. The utility door was behind the open door to the kitchen, and his space was sandwiched in between the office to the west and the ice machine and prep area to the east, with the utility room to his north. The space was only three feet by seven feet but wall man was not a big man, and could move around just fine when he needed to. He had a pillow and a bed and an assortment of old books that he read again and again, as was his custom.

He laundered his clothes and took regular sponge baths and existed solely inside the space except for fifteen minutes a night, each night. He ate little, drank even less, and for the most part made no noise. There was a small register behind the prep station that pulled air into the utility closet, so were there any smells, his were the last to get circulated. He kept quite literally to himself, doing little and thinking much. He had taken to writing recently, the small light from the vent register giving him enough light to see by. The West wall of the office had a window near the ceiling, and during the summer, at around ten, the sun would peek through into the room. He looked forward to that most.

He was quiet. He was clean. He needed almost nothing to live. He had been happy. Up until he ate the tuna.

When the emergency crews came, they had a fine time extracting the man from the space, for he too, had died from the Tuna. Something had been so horrifically wrong with the fish, and it had caused such an extreme reaction in him, that he had voided his bowels as well as retched so hard that he had shed much of his stomach lining in the process.

During the time that the workers were taking everything away, they would turn the TV on and I would be able to check the news. There were stories about Judge Michael Thompson, an elderly man, who had died of food poisoning. He had eaten the same Tuna that Wall Man had. The Judge was one of his faithful and most favorite customers. The Judge's wife, Ruby, had influential friends and when the news of the Tuna and wall man came out, it was over. Roy had been forced to close the restaurant over the incident. He would never work in the food business in Oklahoma again.

The Pond

Craig Atherton looked calmly down at the lake. It was more of a pond but he liked it all the same. The one thing that he couldn't stand was nothing going on. Right now, he had nothing going on.

Nothing going on was like Kryptonite. Not that he actually knew what Kryptonite did. But he figured, if he ever ran into it, this is what it would be like.

He looked at the lake again. It was a round thing, not very big, but he always enjoyed going there. Just a half a mile from the city out on route 14, he drove there almost every Thursday. He had never met the owner but had seen an older fellow once there with a fishing rod late last August. They didn't talk. As soon as Atherton had arrived, the other man packed up his gear and left. As he was driving away he did something peculiar though.

In what appeared to be a 1949 Ford truck, rust colored and beaten he had driven out of the property directly in front of Atherton. With a wink and a nod he said: "Never let them see you cry, my boy." and then he was gone, turning left out onto the road, taking a little dirt with him, enough to leave a trail behind.

Atherton had always wondered about that man. What was he doing fishing in this pond? Atherton had never seen any fish here before. Not even minnows. He had seen plenty of frogs or toad tadpoles and thought that this was the occurrence of the lack of fish. Maybe they were the top of the food chain in the little eco-sphere.

But the old man had appeared a little off in another way. What he had said was the main bother of Atherton's mind. *Never let them see you cry?* Who? Who would be out here to see you cry in the first place? Not the frogs, that's for sure. Not the fish. What fish? And really, he had not seen any other person here as long as he could remember.

And what a memory.

It had been three years since he had been coming here. And now that he put his mind to it, he had never seen anyone even drive down the road.

That was odd.

He guessed he just thought himself lucky is all. As dumb luck would have it and all that. But it did seem odd.

Wait a minute. Why was he thinking about this now? He checked his watch. 5:45 in the afternoon. He had only been here around twenty minutes. Usually this was the time that he left. But not today.

Today he stayed. Who is to say why? Maybe it was just to see what was going to happen. Maybe the mad rush of folks coming home would occur after six and he would leave his suspicions behind and things would get back to normal mentally for him.

He waited.

6:15.

He lay back on the green grass and decided that if indeed, a car were to go by, that it would rouse him. As he drifted off to sleep, he noticed the first crickets beginning to sing.

He awoke as peacefully as he had slept. The first thing that he noticed was that the crickets had stopped. That was odd. It was dark. It was still. The ground was warm still from the sun that day, but the air had taken on a slightly cooler tinge. There was a slight fog lifting from the lake and his car was gone.

His car was what? Gone! Where was his car? He had been seated near the edge of the lake, Sport-coat laid beside him and his 1994 Buick was parked behind him around thirty feet from the gate. But now it was not there.

Not there.

Someone had stolen his car in his sleep.

Dammit! This was just the perfect thing. That car had been everything to him when he had first bought it. His briefcase was in there along with the Jameson account notes. He would be fired. How was he going to get home?

He was standing then. Going back to where the car had been. His shirt stuck to his back in the way that cold wet clothes do when you have been sitting for too long. He tugged it to become untucked. He tightened his belt. He took his glasses from his face and with the left shirt sleeve, cleaned the lenses. He placed his glasses back on his face and pushed them onto his nose with his left index finger.

This was surreal.

He had slept through having my car stolen.

"Dear God", he prayed, "Please let it turn up."

Grabbing his sport-coat from where he had laid it, he started towards the gate to walk down the road towards the highway.

Then he noticed the eyes from the middle of the pond, as large as saucers, watching him.

Cashier

Oh great, it's this guy again. Every night he's here. Come into the store in the middle of the night with nothing more than pajamas and a robe. Sometimes it was slippers; sometimes it was his argyle house shoes. He's sloppy, rude, and you can never tell what he's going to buy. He's never smiled at me once.

It's Halloween tonight and the high school kids are here shopping. Pale faces, fake blood, black spiked hair and leather jackets all looking like the kids in "The Lost Boys." They spotted him down by the organic section and are acting really cool around him. Any minute now....

Yup, they're talking to him, harassing him.

"Shirley, can you come to the front please? Shirley to the front!" I say over the intercom. She's there moments later. She was on the camera watching it all. I did the right thing.

Oh my God, he's screaming! Holy shit, he just threw one of the display tables at them! Grapes and Mandarin oranges are everywhere. Shirley and I are both on the run, screaming at the kids to get out. The kids are screaming too, in actual fright and amusement. The man is on the ground, froth coming out of his mouth, eyes wide, pupils different sizes. He's in spasm like a jackrabbit on an electric fence and then he's... He's not.

His wife is here twenty minutes after the EMT shows up. She had known about the late night adventures. He was a sleepwalker. She also knew of his sanguivoriphobia, his fear of vampires. The EMT says that when he came out of sleep, he suffered a severe epidural hematoma, which caused him to lose balance and crack open his head on the floor.

The wife's eyes were vacant as she walked away.

Unique travels

Say goodbye, she had told me. I always hated that. Saying goodbye I mean. I had always liked her. She had ways that brought out the very best in me. I believe that it was fate that had put us together. Or, perhaps it was God. I have loved her since the first moment that we met so many years ago. Loved her enough to marry her. And now it was over. Now it was all over. It was yesterday.

It was yesterday, like so many years ago. I had been at the church late working on some curriculum for the Sunday school classes. Some pretty good stuff actually. Yawning, I glanced at my watch. Near quitting time already. I was tired and it could wait until morning. I figured I should get home a little early to see how she was doing. Today was grocery day, and she had taken the van so that she could have more room to load in whatever she bought. More room. More money spent. She never did anything halfway. Oh well, that's one of the reasons that I liked her so much. She had class.

Traffic was light and I arrived home in around ten minutes. There was no car outside, but that wasn't anything new. She was probably at Glenda's anyway. I went to get a snack. Strange. No carrots. She hadn't even been home from the grocery store. Something was wrong.

The phone rang.
"Hello?" I said.
"Mr. Hart?" The voice was distant.
"What happened?" I asked before he could tell me.
"Uh, well, Do you have a wife? A Mrs. Heather Hart?"
"Tell me what happened." I repeated, "Now."
"It was in the Supermarket... She's had a stroke."
I paused.
"Mr. Hart?"
"Where are you?" I said.
"At Memorial Hospital Mr. Hart, She's..."

"I'll be right there."
I was there in seven minutes.
She had told me to say goodbye. I always hated that.
Saying goodbye.

Poems

Winding Intelligent
Never Dying
Wind

Down the quiet street,
The wind slowly crept,
Easing its way down,
Through those old
Colonial houses.

The wind spoke
Of an ancient time.
Timeless winds,
Of ancient ones,
Breathing mysteries.

Although changed and polluted,
These winds still blow.
The same ones that blew
In the garden,
With the serpent and the son.

Strange winds reveal things.
My youth. My ignorance.
My uncreative decadence.
Vindictive hot winds
Searing my hardened face,
Turning me to sand.

Oh ancient winged servant;
What have you seen?
What do you know?
Where have you been?

And do you return there soon?

The winds know not change...
But smell, temperature,
Humidity, pollution, pollen content,
Oxygen, Nitrogen, Halogen.
And various dust particles.

Unrelenting, untrusting,
Undermining, undenying,
Unexuberating, unreaching,
Wind, Wind, Wind,
WIND, WIND!

Most knowledgeable of
All gaseous forms...
You, breath of God,
Blew the first of
These small winds.

Tornado, Hurricane, Vortex spinning
Dust devil, Waterspout, Tsunami,
High Pressure, Low Pressure,
Cold Front, Heat Wave, Wind.

God, show your winds
to be all that you would
have them to be...
an elemental force,
in your wonderful creation.

Girl

1

She sat there making a list
onto her notebook

from her cellphone
and scrolling, and scrolling
then a yawn
I wonder if in another life
I could have worked up the nerve
to say hello
nope

She must be waiting for someone
She is waiting
Looking towards me
Sliding off me
like easy butter, looking at the wall
Splot. You can actually hear those eyes
Looking at the empty wall
Her thoughts are empty
Her time is free
She is available
She is bored

I think that I should say hello
to this girl, but how long am I
going to stay in town to get to
know her? Well? What's the
point man? To establish
something that won't last anyway? To begin a non-nonsensical
journey with a sensible soul?
Nope.

Anxious. Quiet. Surreal.
Uninterested. Unwinding.

My mind is lubricated with eye fodder.
She is a vision.
She is a quest
I sojourn
(And sneak glances)
At her...
this...
the...
Holy Grail.

`Thick lips`

Thick lips slur the speech that
breed lies and discrepancies
hypocrisy and lousy statements
of half truth

Thick lips make promises with a forked tongue.

Thick lips kiss well
Thick lips drip poisonous drool
making me nauseated with the stench
of a whores perfume

Thick lips conceal the truth of the vampiric bite
that drains precious life blood

these lips of ours
so thick and supple
are nothing more than slave ships
under no embargo

other than truth

"Spoon!"

I met a boy named Emily
who couldn't do math in his head

I fought a fight named empathy
while he figured out my check

No spoon for tea
some sugar please
oh and you forgot
the cream

Coffee and tea for three
JB and Jesus and me
and our wandering friend
named John

I sometimes think of steak and shake
and how I'd like to learn more

About proper service at a diner
and the etiquette of campers

Coffee tea or me
I can plainly see
your wisdom JB
in ordering the soup

What America said to me

"Plant and grow a garden of happiness in your soul",
was said as I pondered over my life.
"Yes, a garden of love and optimism",

she told me over the phone.

and I got to thinking about a great many number of things...

How would the garden grow?
Where would i keep the roses?
What would I do with the results?
Why have a garden in the first place?

And she said that gardens were nice
And that is where bumblebees live
And children are happy
And all your dreams come true

and that got me thinking again...

Why a garden?
Not a plaza or a nice atrium?
Are gardens that much more important?
Why me? Why my soul?

And she told me that I love people
And that I care
And I bring smiles to her face
And when we talk, I brighten her day

and that made me wonder some more...

Why does she care about my soul?
Why does she talk to me?
Do I really deserve such a nation?
Do I love her as much as she loves me?

And she smiled, and looked away.
And America blushed when I kissed her.
And she told me her pains and sorrows.
And I told her that I cared.

and now I don't wonder anymore...

Ah the run

It wasn't far the run I ran,
just down the block and past the van.
but breathing hard, I came back home
On Becky's birthday, on Saturday.
I sit out front, all alone.
Knowing that wind will make a cool day.

Ah the run, both short and sweet,
ended with my tired feet.
chest a-pounding, head a-thinking,
I need to take a good long bath.
I'm breathing better, I'll bet I'm stinking.
The days of love, I need to laugh.

The days of love, on this cool morning,
The fog has lifted, the birds are soaring.
The days of rain, from Gods green earth.
The trees, the bees, the air so clean.
Ah the run, I think with mirth,
can bind a man, or set him free.

indeed my soul

cherish these moments
under our love
for yours is the kind
worth keeping

Mention to me
words brushed with a kiss

your eyes are the soul
i'm needing

tell me of clouds
that drift thru our lives
they are the nothing
to mountains

live out each second
without hesitation
for yours is a live
worth living

Forever friend

Friends I have had
   friends I have known
But where is the friend
   who has seen me and grown
For friendship it seems
   is seldom indeed
Cause friends are forever
   in want or in need
And you my dear friend
   Who now hold my heart
Shall I never forsake
   and never depart

Oh take me away
   my friend and my love
And sing me the song
   that feels like a hug
And whisper to me
   Your secrets unknown
You are the one
   whom I love and I know

You own my smile
  Forever and true
Here is my heart
  I give it to you

it was like the first time she saw him
leaning over the pool
and gazing in

it was like the very first time
that she saw him
leaning

it was that time that she had the urge
and pushed
she had pushed hard
so hard

and now she had plenty of time
to think about what she did
plenty of time
in c block
in cell 506

plenty of time

Well I know I don't have to die Lord
Cause you died already
You're the pure Lamb
The lamb of God

When my voice is raw
And my fingers are bloody
I know you did it
You did it for

And I praise you
For who you are
Yeah I wanna love you
For everything you've
Ever done for me

But still I'd travel a thousand miles
To be right next to you

Rhymes with Sit

I often wonder about this word @#$%. I't not a word I really understand all that well. We hear of meditarranean Shiatte mushrooms, The Chineese Shitzu dog, and the Muslim Shittes of Iraq, but I am at a complete loss when it comes to our english slang word. What in the world is it, and why is it so powerful?

As a slang word, it is a classic. It has (the obvious) four letters, has a harsh sound, and is in a common reference to something grotesque.and undelightful. So whatever the origin, it is sure to have succeeded, and the word is here to stay, and is probably going to outlast myslef and those reading this book.

The inventor of the common western toilet, our commode, was a fellow by the name of John Crapper. Obviously his name lives in infamy. Throughout the ages of post-commode invention, A toilet is called a John, and when one refers to "taking a crap", they obviously mean that they are going to have a bowel movement.

This brings us to the word crap. We can assume that "crapper" was shortened to "crap", and that the noun was put in play as a verb, and suprisingly enough, is also in reference to the substance itself. How suprising is it that all things in reference to the whole situation get the variable play of the same word.

Ok, so both crap and @#$% are rude and usually unacceptable to say in most knitting circles. That was the previous age. Today you can almost say them anywhere. Oh, I recant. You can say "Crap" almost anywhere. "@#$%" on the otherhand is still making it's evolution into the silver screen, and into everyday life. These great words are both nouns and verbs, and are in every english-speaking household in the U.S. (whether the households admit to them or not). You can hear both of them on any major city radio station, and on most densly populated street corners in the land.

So what differentiates these tow words? One can argue that there is no difference whatsoever, and that they hold the same weight. Of course there are some holes in that reasoning, seeing that the FCC has banned the use of our topic word, @#$%, from every brodcast Telivision station from here to Nome, Alaska. If you want to hear the word on the set, you've got to pay for it.

If dor instance our dear Mr. Crapper had been named Mr. @#$%er, we would see "Crap" as the repulsing word today that we see @#$% being. But we have the way that it is, and we must deal with it.

Every culture has it's own "taboo" and it puts the comfortability zone around it's familiarity. We have these zones to hem in our sense of what is right and wrong, to place borders of trust and "niceness" around us, so that we are a balance culture. We feel secure, and in doing so, we are more reasonable, and in doing so stay inside the walls of sanity. But in the same way that we have these degrees of self-respect, we also hold the opposite to be true... we just don't admit it openly.

You can find underground publications, XXX videos, questionable literature anywhere you go in this fine nation; if you but try hard enough. There is a mischeviousness that we all assert when we feel that we can get away with it. We get a strange sense of joy in throwing in "naughty" words every time we get an excuse. Jokes around the stereotypical watercooler at the stereotypical white collar job... On the cigarette break on the stereotypical blue collar job... There is a secret and quite relieving pleasure at breaking taboos, even if just for the moment.

We have examined the history of the word. We have seen it's many uses, it's boundries and the word within the culture. What else is there to say? A lot probably. We could go into the whos, whys, and whats listed in the dictionary. History, literature, or possibly talk about the resurrgance of the word within the hippie culture... But hey! If I went on for hours, you would get tired and bored, and, honestly, who really wants to hear that @#$%?

Pilate knew it was going t to be a long day when the Jews were already clamoring at his terrace. "Oh great Caesars! What is it now?" He must have been in a terrible mood. But who could blame him. What a rotten office to be given. Jerusalem... the supposed city of peace. Instead, to him, it was a city of nightmares.

Are you a king?

He knew who Joshua Ben Joseph was. He had heard of him when he cleansed the temple. He had also known about the centurions tales of his servant. He had known about Ben Josephs entrance into the city just days before, and he knew very well about Ben Josephs cousin, John Baptist. Now Pilate just wanted to know the truth. Was this Joshua like the Joshua of old or not? Was he the redeemer, the Christ?

You say correctly that I am a King...

Everyone who is in the truth hears my voice...

That was all he had needed, So, leaning forward in his chair... straining and searching the condemned mans face, he said:

What is truth?

Pilate declared him perfect.

The translation goes: "I find no fault in him at all."

None? Apparently Pilate was sold on the matter.

"Look, here he is, I am giving him over to you but know this: I do not find any fault in him. He is perfect."

To prove his point, he made a sign to spite them. It read: "Jesus of Nazareth. King of the Jews." It was written in three languages. The King.

Pilate had switched allegiances. Though he was not a Jew, he realized something powerful. Something true. Jesus as king. Jesus was more powerful than Pilate could ever be, and he could not compete with that. His wife had even told him that.

Pilate is like you or I. We desperately want to find something wrong with Christ so that we may denounce him. Anything. We cannot. We find him perfect every time. We want to be better than him. But we are not. We cannot even compete. We are left with two choices. Release him, or crucify him.

It all boils down to this. Every person that I have talked to has some grievance against Christianity in one respect or another. But no one I know has a problem with Jesus. Our only problem arises when it comes time to do something with Christ. What is he to us? Is it our part-time thing? Our Sunday Jesus? Or is he the risen King, the Lord of all Lords?

You see, it differs for every man. I do not know the stipulations that are on your life, but I do know this... To one man, he said that he must be born again. Another man was told by him to sell everything that he had and then he would be perfect. But to everyone of his disciples, and to you and I today, he tells us to follow him. He will not turn you away. As the scripture says: "Anyone who calls upon the name of the Lord shall be saved."

What a simple concept. Following Jesus. What simpler way to lead others than to follow someone in front of you. A good scout follows a path. A good leader follows those that have gone on before him. Lost you may feel, but follow Him, and all will be well.

Ask and you will receive, seek and you will find, knock, and the door will be opened for you. Follow and you will arrive. Through the cry, the pain, and the goodness. Through the valley of Baca. Through being a witness to the ends of the Earth. Follow Christ and him only.

My friend, my dearest reader, if you follow Jesus with all that is in your heart, you will arrive at truth. We all go from strength to strength. We all go from glory to glory. We will all appear before God in Zion, if we but follow him. He knows you, and he knows your troubles. There are six billion people on this planet and yet, he knows all of us! What a God to love me for who I am. Not because I am doing anything important… but just because I am here.

Ok. Maybe you followed Him, and you felt lead astray. Maybe you gave in. Maybe you felt that the valley was too deep and dark, and you let go. Maybe you quit. It is not too late to start back to him. No one ever succeeds at running away from their problems. Problems always have on better running shoes than us. Pray this prayer from your heart. If it doesn't seem real enough, then make something up. Just be real with God. He wants you to be one with Him today.

The Interwebs and the TheFacebook.com

I dove deeper and deeper into these new unearthed mysteries and came upon the "Archon Invasion" series by Rob Skiba. All of the information that I had gathered together by myself with Empires and Generals and my novel was now here in one lump. That the whole earth had flooded to destroy ancient bloodlines of a cursed seed of mankind was the crux of the teaching. The Nephilim represented, and after that, the Canaanites and their kind represented the cursed fallen angel bloodline that YHVH must purge from the earth to make a pure race once again. It was strange and fresh but it resonated with all of my research and made sense. But if only Rob looked passed the demi-gods into the past to discover why earth was so important. And then it happened. Rob Skiba posted a flat earth teaching asking if it was possible. Well of course it was, but not very popular.

Christians everywhere blew gaskets. People from all walks of Christendom came to attack him and everything he had ever stood for. He left Facebook and took down his homepage and disappeared for a while. I created a Facebook group in response to this: "Rob Skiba is Incredible" and posted a couple of his more important (so I thought) videos. I ran the page anonymously (until right now) and was astonished to see so much hatred and vitriol towards him. It was in front of them all the time, yet they still denied it and clung to their globes and spheres and planets. It was a sad epoch in Facebook history. Since then, Rob has come back to Facebook and his home website is now up and running again. I smiled when I found out. He's a good guy, and, while I've not agreed with everything he's taught, his flat earth and antediluvian (pre-flood) messages seemed scripturally sound and balanced.

After I found Rob's stuff at the beginning of 2014, I started looking for flat earth videos. There were a couple out there at first and then a guy named Eric Dubay posted several that really caught my attention, and then published a video called: "200 proofs earth is not a spinning ball" in October of 2015. I rejoiced that someone had some common sense to promote other people's findings of their common sense and their scientific experiments. Since that time, I have done nothing but sit back in amazement as more and more people flock to the truth as the Bible tells it. That: "For God so loved the world that He gave His one and only Son."

I've been on Facebook off and on since they released it. More off than on since my alma mater never bothered to sign up to be a "college" so I had to wait for the public version to come out. I've been banned twice for shenanigans and tomfoolery. Both, I contest, were under duress. I guess I couldn't treat Facebook like Myspace. Well, I guess you can now, but you couldn't back then. It was pretty harsh back in the early days but now it's slid into the funk of the slough of despond, as mentioned in <u>Pilgrim's Progress</u>. No matter. My tale begins almost a year ago at the end of June on Facebook. I posted something about Genesis 1:1 pointing to a separation of systems. "In the beginning, God created the heavens and the earth." In Hebrew, heaven means sky and earth means land. So it made sense to me, as a mad genius, to spell that out for people.

Let's hold on for a second. You've most probably read in the previous chapters how I proceed to explain in great detail, my journey in my mind and my heart into the Flat earth understanding. Well. Sure. On the MBTI scale I score a 90% INTP, with a little E making me do things out in public. So you can understand, if you know anything about the Myers and Briggs test, how hard it is for someone like me to accept anything right off the bat. I have to go over and over and over all the information like a giant herbivorous behemoth chews grass. It isn't until I've sucked all the juices out of something that I am ready to swallow it. Very irksome to others, but once I've swallowed it... I will hold on to the bitter end before letting go.

Wait. Where was I? Oh yeah. I posted my first flat earth post on Facebook about a year ago. That was a trip. Now, truth be told, I've done a lot more digging into other weird Biblical teachings that I had on the flat earth teaching. I, you know… "Knew it" sure, but I just had never understood why it would be important. As a matter of fact, it kinda pissed me off. I was going to be a science fiction writer after all, you know? Why the heckfire should I care about the frikkin shape of the earth? What difference did it make? Why don't you leave me alone about this? I already *know* it's *flat*. I don't need to talk about it too. I'm too busy writing about Krampus.

But the more I told God that it wasn't important to my life at the moment, the more I was convicted that the time was now. I recall after a day's worth of research in Baalbek stones, worldwide pyramids and sunken cities that I just put my head in my hands and thought: "Why does it always comes back to the flat earth?" I was convinced that there was another cornerstone to uncover. I was convinced at that time that I could find something else. I was sure that Pangea was the root, or Eden was the root, or the Deluge, or Antediluvian mankind, or something… But the more I gave it time to sink in, the more I realized that Christ was right in Luke 12:56,57: "Hypocrites! You know how to discern the surface of the earth and of the sky, but how do you not know to discern this time? And why do you not even judge for yourselves what is right?" I was wrong, so wrong about everything. If the key to understanding prophetic wisdom from the scriptures was based upon an understanding of nature itself I was in big trouble. First I needed to look at God's work to understand the future of God's work.

That catches me up to today. And that, my friends, is my flat earth story. At least it is from 1981 until now. There's a lot you don't need to know and a lot that I could have added. But the finalization of my quest into leaning not on my own understanding but acknowledging *HIM* has come to this point with me. The Hebrew model earth, or flat earth, or whatever you want to call it, has consumed my being with truth and infused my mind with a deeper foundation into the Holy Scriptures, and indeed The Word itself. Point being, We're here now at the end of the book and I still haven't really given you any Bible verses to study, or any proofs you can do on your own to show that you are learning and growing and are "studying to show yourself approved before God and man." The good news is, that this is only the first part of this collection. If you want to skip to the end, there's a whole cornucopia of scriptures to dig into right now... But first, Todd Monachello would like to know where you stand with all of this information.

www.ingramcontent.com/pod-product-compliance
Lightning Source LLC
Chambersburg PA
CBHW030153200626
46812CB00016B/1829